CALUMET CITY PUBLIC LIBRARY

3 1613 00339 2753

P9-BYO-716

THIS IS A BORZOI BOOK PUBLISHED
BY ALFRED A. KNOPF
Copyright © 2001, 2003 by
Hachette Livre All rights
reserved under International and
Pan-American Copyright
Conventions. Published in the United
States of America by Alfred A.
Knopf, a division of Random House,
Inc., New York, and simultaneously in
Canada by Random House of Canada
Limited, Toronto. Distributed by
Random House, Inc., New York.
Originally published in France as La petite
soeur de Lisa by Hachette Jeunesse in 2001.
KNOPF, BORZOI BOOKS, and the colophon are
registered trademarks of Random House, Inc.
www.randomhouse.com/kids
Library of Congress Cataloging-in-Publication
Gutman, Anne.[Petite soeur de Lisa. English.]
Lisa's baby sister / Anne Gutman, Georg
Hallensleben.—1st Borzoi Books ed.
p. cm.—(Misadventures of Gaspard and Lisa)
Summary: Lisa is very unhappy about the
arrival of her new baby sister.
ISBN 0-375-82251-8 [1. Babies—Fiction.
2. Sisters—Fiction. 3. Behavoir—Fiction.]
I. Hallensleben, Georg. II. Title. III. Series.
PZ7.G9844 L1 2003 [Fic]—dc21 2002001999
First Borzoi Books edition: March 2003
Printed in France
10 9 8 7 6 5 4 3 2 1

ANNE GUTMAN · GEORG HALLENSLEBEN

Lisa's Baby Sister

Alfred A. Knopf ✒ New York

CALUMET CITY PUBLIC LIBRARY

My mom has been pregnant for a very long time, and I am tired of it. She can't run to catch the bus. She makes me carry my own schoolbag.

She's too fat to play on the seesaw with me.
There's a baby in her belly, and I don't like it.

My parents haven't
decided on a name yet.

I told them I have some good names:
Doofus for a girl
or Goofus for a boy.
My dad told me to go to my room.

My best friend, Gaspard, promised me
that he would NEVER talk to the baby.
And we could pretend that it didn't exist.

But then it happened.
We were leaving school . . .

. . . and there was my grandma with a big smile. "The baby will be born today," she told me. "While we wait, we'll have some ice cream."

Grandma ordered a gigantic ice cream
with two little umbrellas for me.
"Lisa," she said, "when you were born . . ."

But I'd heard it before, the story of
Victoria, my big sister. She was very
jealous and she vowed never to talk to me.
But now Victoria talks to me all the time,
even when cartoons are on.

The ice cream was melting all over the table when Grandma's cell phone rang. She became very excited and she said, "It's a girl! Her name is Lila."

That night, Dad came home without the baby or Mom, but with lots of photos. I didn't want to look at them.

Two days later, Mom finally came home. And the
baby, too. Victoria invited some friends over so
she could show off Lila. It was as if they had
never seen a baby. All the baby did was eat,
but they kept saying, "Oh, isn't she cute!"

To annoy them, I played my flute
really loud just outside
the baby's room.

CALUMET CITY PUBLIC LIBRARY

That made Victoria angry with
me, and we started fighting.

But the baby began to cry, so Victoria let go of me. She and her friends stayed in the baby's room all day. They even took more photos. And then I heard Victoria's blond friend say that Lila and I have the same nose and that we look a lot alike.

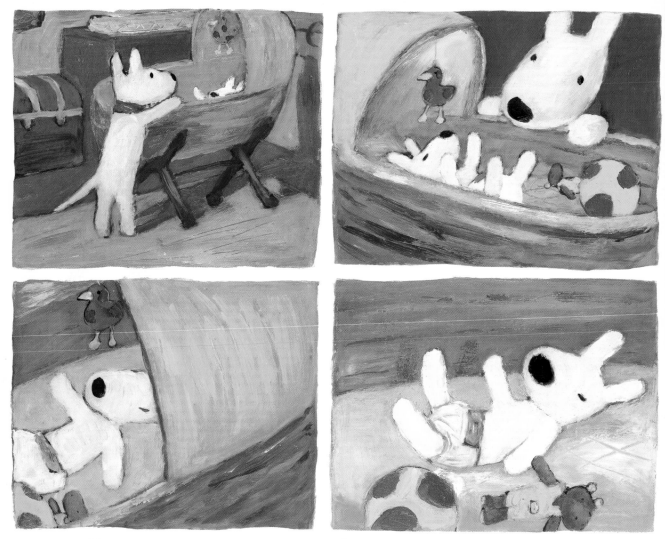

When everyone left, I went in to look at
the baby. She had a tiny nose that twitched
in her sleep. Actually, she looked like my old
teddy bear, Elliot, only a little cleaner.

She looked content, even when I opened her
eyelid to see what color her eyes were.

I picked her up.
She was so little!

And she smelled
very nice.

The next day, I helped my parents push her carriage around the square. Gaspard wanted to help, too, but she's MY little sister!

As we strolled around the square,
I got a great idea.

I'll take Lila to school tomorrow for show and tell. Then everyone will see that I have the cutest little sister in the world! It will be great for Mom, too. It will give her a rest from taking care of Lila.

And that way Mom will
have enough time . . .

. . . to finally finish making my
Tyrannosaurus rex costume.